My Ireland COUNTING Book

Illustrated by Eoin Ryan

THE O'BRIEN PRESS
DUBLIN

ONE

1

One stone castle

in the Irish countryside

TWO

2

Two Irish wolfhounds

having a great time

THREE

3

Three bodhráns

making a lot of noise

FOUR

4

Four thatched cottages

in an Irish village

FIVE
5

Five tin whistles

playing a lively tune

SIX

6

Six currachs

heading out to sea

SEVEN

7

Seven Connemara

ponies in a race

EIGHT

8

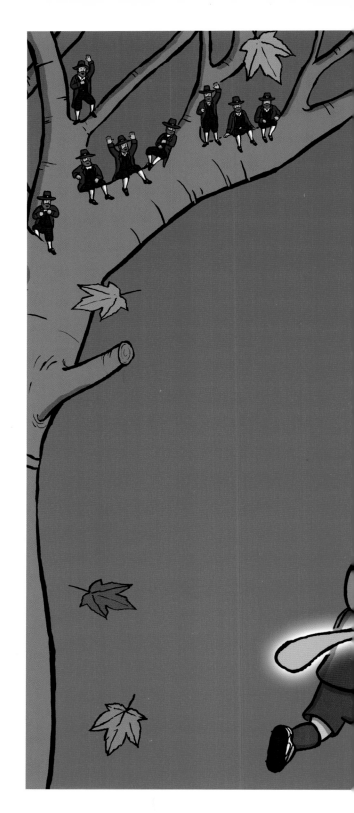

Eight hurleys

trying to hit the ball

NINE

Nine Irish flags

waving in the breeze

TEN

Ten Irish dancers

dancing a jig

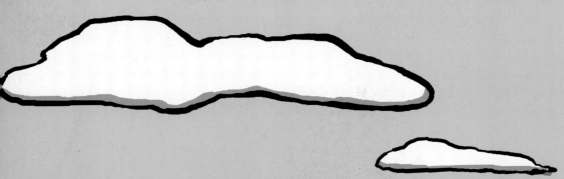

This picture shows the things you have counted:
a castle, an Irish wolfhound, a bodhrán, a thatched cottage, a tin whistle,
currachs, hurleys, a flag, a dancer … but something is missing!
Can you work out what it is?

1 Irish castle

Castles are found all over Ireland. They were built hundreds of years ago and are made of stone. People usually lived upstairs in the castle, as this was safest. There were lots of small cottages and workshops around the castle for craftspeople, such as blacksmiths and weavers, and their families. There was also a wall around the castle for defence.

Irish wolfhound

2 The Irish wolfhound is one of the tallest dog breeds. They are very gentle dogs. Originally they were used for hunting wolves. They have short lives, between five and ten years. The breed has been known in Ireland for several thousand years, but long ago, only kings and nobles could own these dogs. Nowadays wolfhounds are often used as mascots, and you will see them leading parades of soldiers or firefighters in many countries.

Bodhrán

3 The bodhrán (pronounced *bow-rawn*) is a drum. It's made of animal skin stretched on a wooden hoop. You play it with a stick or with your hand. It can have a dead sound if it gets damp – that's why you'll often see bodhrán players holding their instrument near the open fire to dry it out. This makes the sound nice and lively. The instrument has been known and used for many hundreds of years in Ireland.

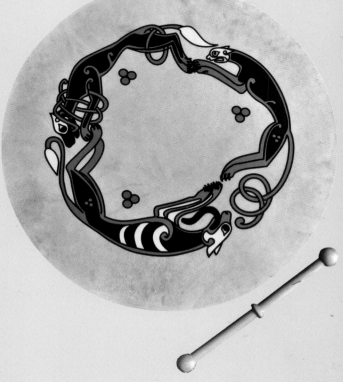

Thatched cottage

4

A thatched cottage has a roof made of straw. The straw is very thick. It keeps the house nice and warm and dry. But it has to be replaced every ten to fifteen years or so. When it's new, it is a lovely golden colour. Sometimes birds (or other creatures) might make their nests in it!

5 ## Tin whistle

The tin whistle has six holes. You cover them all first, then lift up each finger, one at a time, for each note. You can play two octaves on it – you blow harder for the higher octave. You can play simple tunes or very difficult ones. Some people can play very, very fast on the tin whistle.

Currach

6 The currach is a lightweight boat made of animal skin or canvas stretched over a wooden frame. It was used by fishermen in the west of Ireland until recent years. Fishermen turned them upside down on the beach to dry them. When moving them from place to place, they looked very funny – like large insects – walking under the boats with only their legs sticking out. Nowadays currach races are held off the west and south coasts of Ireland.

Connemara pony

7 The Connemara pony is a breed that originated in Ireland. They are strong, lively, intelligent and easily trained. Very athletic, they are good jumpers and also make very good show ponies, and can be ridden by both children and adults. Connemara pony shows are held all over the world, but the most famous is the one held in Clifden, County Galway, every year.

Hurley

8 A hurley is used in the game of hurling. It's made from ash wood because ash has a good spring, or bounce, in it. It's about waist high. Players may hit the ball (called a *sliotar*) on the ground and in the air, and they will leap very high to hit it with their hurleys. They also hit a moving ball, often at great speed. Hurling is a very exciting game, one of the fastest games in the world.

9 Irish flag

The Irish flag has three colours: green, white and orange. It is a tricolour. The green represents the Republic of Ireland. The orange represents the Protestant tradition in Northern Ireland. The white stands for peace between the two traditions. It was designed in the nineteenth century.

Irish dancer 10

Irish dancers begin to learn their steps at a young age. They dance reels, jigs and hornpipes, as well as group dances like sets. Irish dancing is very energetic! With their feet, dancers tap out the rhythm to tunes played on various instruments. The body is held quite straight, the arms stiff by the sides. Irish dancers usually wear very colourful clothes and have curly hair that bounces when they jump. The popular show *Riverdance* has made modern Irish dancing famous all over the world.

Here's how we say the numbers in Irish:

1 - aon

2 - dó

3 - trí

4 - ceathair

5 - cúig

6   - sé

7   - seacht

8   - ocht

9   - naoi

10 - deich

This edition first published 2017 by The O'Brien Press Ltd,
12 Terenure Road East, Rathgar, Dublin 6, Ireland.
Tel: +353 1 4923333; Fax: +353 1 4922777
E-mail: books@obrien.ie
Website: www.obrien.ie
First published 2011.

The O'Brien Press is a member of Publishing Ireland.

ISBN: 978-1-84717-931-9

10 9 8 7 6 5 4 3 2 1
21 20 19 18 17

Printed in Drukarnia Skleniarz, Poland.
The paper used in this book is produced using pulp from managed forests

Published in
DUBLIN
UNESCO
City of Literature